The question is, can the cat count?

First published in Great Britain in 1997 by
Jarrold Publishing
Whitefriars, Norwich NR3 1TR

ISBN 0-7117-0977-7

Printed by Proost, Belgium 1/97

THE UNIVERSE OF ADRIAN COX

Well Charlie, they don't appear to have any bitey bums, will a postman's leg do?

...So remember, when you want to get attention, go for the razorblades and ketchup...

... Nah mate, that one's the computer, these are the manuals...

You're lucky, it's only your legs they're after

Rex and shep watched from the bushes as the black sheep plotted to foil their chances at the sheepdog trials

How many times have I got to tell you?
Don't play with your food

...Be prepared for all kinds of equipment failure...

... I can assure you Mrs. Blenkinsop, the computer will not be taking your place in accounts.

It's raining cats... Just cats!!!

Early man's first attempt at intelligent communication

Wow Jacques, a real fish-eye lens!

Stop following me around, you're like
a flock of sheep

Umbrella salesmen taking raindance lessons

Looks like you'll have to take him for a walk now

...and now I'd like to introduce you to the Architect of the world wide web...

The location of the new cat flap shed a whole new light on his master's feelings for him

Course I can't understand him, he's a bloody frog!

Quick! Fetch the sheepdog!

The dragon entering her lair

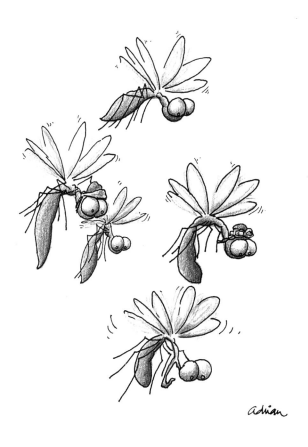

Hey! Hey! Shiny car on the freeway
at 1 o'clock – Dive! Dive! Dive!

Suddenly Vladimir realised he'd left his
magnetic chess set beside the compass

Damn cats playing those kazoos again

Early man's first attempt at subtle sexual advances

O.K. Nobody move! We've come for
the French.

On hearing the postman approaching, Henry reached for his bone crunching teeth...

Pop upped and buckled on his peacemaker,
the kids were getting too rowdy in the backroom

The self-service fast food counter

Relax Bill, he's just a pointer

Hey lookee here Buz, sled tracks

George practises his dragon slaying
while she's out shopping

... Data security can sometimes be a problem ...

... It seems that our clever little William has managed to hack into your private mailbox.

The males spend two months carefully nurturing their eggs.

Well, hell yes Miss Witherspoon, we did advertise
for a headhunter, show him in

... won't swallow anything too big,
she's worried about getting stretch marks

He's out there with "The Big Book of Insects", trying to decide what's stuck to the front of his new car

Mary! Ellen! Put your heads back on this minute

Early woman selects the material
for her new fur coat

Computer experts are generally in short supply . . .

The office would like to know if sir is available for work today.

Bagged the blighter in the fireplace last Christmas

..... and of course kids, we don't have to look very far to find another species where a large voracious female devours the male ...

You're lucky, it's only your legs they're after